CORAL REEF VIEWS

VICKI DELANY

ORCA BOOK PUBLISHERS

Library and Archives Canada Cataloguing in Publication

Title: Coral reef views / Vicki Delany.
Names: Delany, Vicki, 1951– author.
Series: Rapid reads.
Description: Series statement: Rapid reads

Identifiers: Canadiana (print) 20190168846 | Canadiana (ebook) 20190168854 |
ISBN 9781459822955 (softcover) | ISBN 9781459823501 (PDF) |
ISBN 9781459823518 (EPUB)

Classification: LCC PS8557.E4239 C67 2020 | DDC C813/.6—dc23

Library of Congress Control Number: 2019943959
Simultaneously published in Canada and the United States in 2020

Summary: In this work of crime fiction, paramedic Ashley Grant
helps her visiting father solve the mystery of a missing neighbor.

*Orca Book Publishers is committed to reducing the consumption
of nonrenewable resources in the making of our books. We make
every effort to use materials that support a sustainable future.*

Orca Book Publishers gratefully acknowledges the support for its publishing
programs provided by the following agencies: the Government of Canada,
the Canada Council for the Arts and the Province of British Columbia
through the BC Arts Council and the Book Publishing Tax Credit.

Design by Ella Collier
Cover photography by gettyimages.ca/Jeffery Richards

ORCA BOOK PUBLISHERS
orcabook.com

Printed and bound in Canada.

23 22 21 20 • 4 3 2 1

To my mother, a teacher

ONE

MY FATHER DOESN'T do vacations well. It's hard for him to relax. He'd rather be working in the garage, puttering about fixing things, or taking care of the garden. He also likes to help around the house. When he does that, my mother follows him, putting things back where they belong.

He didn't want to retire. But when he realized he was being offered a retirement package instead of being laid off, he took the package.

He wanted to go to on a cross-continent RV trip, but my mother had always dreamed of a Caribbean beach vacation.

Mom won.

At the moment I'm living and working in a Caribbean tourist destination. So here they are in the Victoria and Albert Islands. Visiting me.

Mom's loving it. The hot sun, the cool sand, the warm ocean. Relaxing in a lounge chair with a book on her lap and a cold drink by her side. Getting up now and again to splash in the waves or swim in the pool.

Dad's bored.

He doesn't read, and he doesn't relax. He doesn't like the food here much. He's not fond of fish, or so he says. He seems to like fish when my mom cooks it at home.

I took a couple of days off work to spend some time with them. I wanted to show them around Grand Victoria Island, which I now call home.

That took about half a day. Then we stopped at Club Louisa, one of the nicest hotels on the island. Mom and I had conch fritters and margaritas under umbrellas on the patio restaurant and enjoyed a swim in the infinity pool.

Dad had a burger and a beer inside, where he could catch a football game on the big-screen TV.

The next day we went on a boat tour in the morning and snorkeled in the afternoon. Mom loved being out on the water. She also loved the attention of the handsome young tour guide who showed her how to breathe underwater. Dad talked to the captain about football. He checked the weather forecast on his phone and worried that the driveway at home wouldn't get shoveled.

Tuesday I went back to work. I left Mom making breakfast and planning a morning on the beach followed by a walk to a beachside hotel for lunch. Dad was reading the weather report for Toronto again. "Another two feet of snow tonight. I told you we shouldn't have left, Donna. I don't trust that guy you hired. I'll have a heck of a mess to clean up."

"He'll do a fine job, dear." Mom flipped the bacon.

I gave her a kiss and headed out. I'd called my regular cabbie to come and pick me up. I'm lucky enough to live in a small vacation complex. While I waited I popped into the office to say good morning to Darlene, the day manager.

I found her slamming down the phone, her face twisted into a dark cloud. She is about my age and very attractive, with big dark eyes and perfect bone structure. Her hair is shaved down to the scalp on one side and tied into long braids on the other. The look suits her.

"Problem?" I asked.

"Ashley, good morning. Sorry about that." She gave me a weak smile. "Nothing I can't handle. Actually, it is something I can't handle, which is why I need a plumber. We've got a broken pipe somewhere in building two, and the ground-floor units are flooding. George and Philip are running around with buckets, but they're having trouble keeping up. I've been trying everyone I know, but they all say they can't come for hours yet."

"You need a plumber? You're in luck. My dad's a plumber."

A spark of interest showed in her black eyes. "He is?"

"Fully licensed and employed as such until he retired a couple of months ago. I'll go get him."

The spark faded. "I can't ask him to work on his vacation," Darlene said.

"Believe me," I said. "He'll thank you. My mother will thank you."

"I don't know that I can pay Canadian rates. Whatever they are."

"Don't worry about that. He'll pay you to let him do it."

"He's not enjoying his vacation?"

"When my mom said she wants to stay longer next time, I heard him mutter the word *divorce*."

We both looked up at the sound of a car horn. I waved to Henry, the taxi driver. "I'll get Dad and meet you at building two. He doesn't have any of his tools, but he can make an assessment of what you need and maybe do a temporary fix."

Darlene leaped up from behind her desk. "Unit twelve is the worst."

I went to the taxi and asked Henry to wait. He leaned back in his seat and pulled out his phone. I ran upstairs and explained the situation to Dad. He got to his feet so fast he almost knocked his chair over.

"Aren't you going to finish your break-fast?" Mom asked.

"It can wait," he replied, heading for the door.

If Darlene's problem turned out to be nothing, I might have to go to some of the other hotels on the island and sabotage their plumbing.

Dad charged off to building two, a man on a mission. I headed for the cab and another day in the ambulance.

TWO

MY SHIFT WAS busy. The near-drowning of a Japanese tourist who couldn't swim but thought he'd dive into the deep end anyway. A fender bender caused by an American who rented a car but forgot we drive on the left-hand side of the road here. A couple of locals in a bar brawl—at ten o'clock in the morning. A call came in from one of our "frequent flyers"—a lonely old man who used a ride in the ambulance and a chat with the hospital nurses as his regular social outing. I'd once suggested he join the bridge club in his apartment building. He told me he didn't like any of the members.

We'd been busy, but I managed to get off shift in time. I found my mom reading in the shade of a royal palm on my small private patio. I gave her a kiss on the top of her head and asked, "Where's Dad?"

"At work."

"Work? You mean working on the plumbing? That's taken all day?"

"No, but he decided all the taps needed inspection. He's been doing that."

I laughed. "I've invited a friend to join us for dinner. I'll find Dad and let him know."

"A friend. That's nice."

"My friend's a Canadian police officer who's working with the V&A police. I thought Dad would enjoy having a man to talk to."

Mom's eyes opened wide. "A man?"

"Yes."

"A man? As in a gentleman friend?"

"A man. As in a friend who happens to be a man."

"Oh," she said, trying to hide her disappointment. I'm the youngest of four daughters, the only one not married. Even with three sons-in-law and ten grandchildren, Mom still has hopes for me.

"I'll go find Dad," I said. "We're meeting Alan at seven."

I headed over to building two. Four buildings make up the complex where I live. It's pretty nice, with two pools, beautiful gardens, walkways and a thirty-second walk to the beach. I was about to phone Dad to ask where he was when I heard his laugh.

I smiled to myself. My dad has a deep, rolling laugh, the sort that makes everyone around him laugh too. I hadn't heard that laugh much on this visit.

I found him sitting under a palm tree, beer in hand, with a man about his age.

"Hi," I said.

Dad's new friend stood up.

"Paul," Dad said. "This is my daughter, Ashley. Ashley, meet Paul Saunders."

Paul thrust out his hand. He was a big guy, tall and broad with a shock of curly gray hair and a deep tan. He wore baggy shorts, a Toronto Blue Jays ball cap and an Ottawa Senators T-shirt. His handshake was warm and friendly. "Frank's been telling me all about you," he said. "How are you enjoying living on Grand Victoria?"

"It's different," I said. "The work is challenging but interesting. Did you fix the problem, Dad?"

"Got that leak shut off with no problem at all. But the pipes here aren't in good shape, so I gave them all a once-over." He shook his head. "I told your friend in the office she better see to that right quick before the whole place is underwater."

"I'm sure she appreciated your help," I said. "I came to tell you we're going to dinner at six forty-five."

He lifted his beer bottle. "Water," he said to Paul, "is a dangerous thing when it's where it isn't supposed to be."

* * *

My friend Alan Westbrook is an RCMP officer on temporary assignment with the local police. The Victoria and Albert Islands is a small country in the Western Caribbean. It's made up of numerous islands, many of which are uninhabited. I've been to concerts where there are more people than this entire country has. Grand Victoria is the biggest and most populated island. But it's not more than sixty square kilometers in area and just four kilometers wide at the broadest place. It's still a British colony, now mostly self-governing. It's a major tourist destination, and the tiny local population can't support it all. So plenty of Canadian and British people work here. Like Alan and me.

Alan and I are…I don't quite know what Alan and I are. I like him. He seems to like me. I'm a paramedic and he's a cop. This is a small island, so we bump into each other at work a lot. We've been out a couple of times. To casual dinners or to a bar to hear local music. But nothing more than that, and nothing has ever been said about it becoming more.

I noticed my mom studying him. Clearly she approved—he's a good-looking man, tall and fit with hair streaked golden by the sun, a huge smile and warm blue eyes. He gave her no signs that he and I were more than friends.

My dad seemed to like him a lot. Or maybe he just liked having the chance to talk to someone new. He asked about policing in the islands. Alan told him the funny stories. He didn't mention that Grand Victoria, like everywhere, has its dark side.

The restaurant we'd chosen was a casual place right on the beach. The sun was setting as we arrived. Torches lined the walkway. The tables were lit by candles in hurricane lamps. Lights from boats in the harbor rose and fell on the gentle waves. The surf murmured lightly as it touched the beach.

It was a nice evening, and I was glad to see Dad enjoying himself. He even agreed to try the restaurant's specialty, conch chowder.

* * *

Dad's good mood didn't last long. When I got home from work on Wednesday, my parents were playing cards. I gave them each a kiss and went to change out of my uniform.

"I'll go and check, see if he's in yet. Maybe he forgot his phone," Dad said.

"Don't badger the man, Frank," Mom said.

I heard the door open and shut.

"What's the matter?" I asked Mom.

She let out a long breath. "Your father was supposed to be meeting his new friend Paul for lunch. Paul didn't show. So your father spent the entire afternoon trying to find something to do." She gathered up the cards. "A woman can only play so many hands of gin."

"Feel like a walk?" I asked.

"Sure."

* * *

We had a long, lovely walk along the beach. When we got back, Dad was playing solitaire at the dining-room table.

"I'll cook tonight, if you like," I said. "I can do chicken on the barbecue and make a salad."

"He's not home and not answering his phone," Dad said.

"Who's not home?"

"Paul."

"Leave the man alone, Frank," Mom said. "He went out for the day and forgot he'd made plans with you."

"He's not the sort to forget."

"You don't know what sort he is," Mom said. "You only met him yesterday."

"I left a note on his door to call me when he gets in."

"I'm ready for a glass of wine," Mom said. "I hope we get another beautiful sunset like yesterday."

* * *

By the time I left for work the next morning, Paul still hadn't called. Dad was getting ill-tempered, and Mom annoyed. "The man has a life, Frank. He might have met people. Made friends." Mom glanced at me and wiggled her eyebrows. "Maybe even a lady friend."

"Have a nice day." I grabbed the bagged lunch Mom had made for me. It was like being back in school.

I was enjoying that lunch—cold tomato soup and a ham sandwich—when Dad called.

"I need you to contact the hospital for me," he said.

"Are you okay? Where's Mom?"

"She's gone to the beach. I'm fine, but I'm worried about Paul. Maybe he's had an accident."

"Dad."

"I called the hospital, and they said they had no one of that name. He might be unconscious or using another name. You can find out, can't you? It's got to be a small hospital."

"Yes, it's a small hospital." That was an understatement. "But…"

"If he's not there, ask your friend Alan. The police wouldn't talk to me, but he can get things moving."

"Dad! I'll speak to someone at the hospital next time I'm there, but I can't tell Alan to get the police involved. Your friend is an adult. He can go away for a couple of days if he wants to."

"But we were going to have lunch yesterday. Today he was going to take me to the conch farm. He said it's an interesting operation."

"Dad…"

"I asked Darlene, and she said he's booked the room for another two weeks. I…uh…just happened to be passing when the maid went in to clean, and I peeked in."

"Dad!"

"His stuff all seems to be there. Two suitcases are in the closet."

"You don't know what stuff he has. Maybe he brought three suitcases."

"No one travels with three suitcases. Not with airline baggage fees what they are these days. Ashley, can you do this for me? Please. I have a bad feeling about this."

I sighed. My dad didn't ask me for much. "Okay, I'll call the hospital, and I'll contact the police about any John Does." Meaning unidentified males. "If I find out he's with a girlfriend, I'm not going to tell you where."

"I just need to know, honeybunch. Thanks."

Reluctantly I put down my sandwich. There really is nothing like a Mom-made lunch. Feeling slightly embarrassed, I made the calls. No one knew anything about a man matching Paul's description.

* * *

When I got home, I found Mom reading by the pool. I dropped into the lounge chair next to her. I tilted my face toward the hot sun. "Another book?" I asked.

"A novel a day," she said. "The perfect vacation."

"Where's Dad?"

She put down the book. "Not having the perfect vacation. He called a taxi and has gone into town."

I didn't like the tone in her voice. "Why? What's wrong with that?"

"He's still worried about his friend. Paul told him about some beach bar he likes. Frank's gone to check it out. See if he's there."

"Jeez, Mom. Didn't it occur to Dad that Paul might not have thought having lunch with some guy from Toronto was important? Or that he's gone off to do whatever he wants to do?"

"I tried telling him that, Ashley. But you know your father. When he gets an idea in his head…"

"I know."

"He's so dreadfully bored here. He asked Darlene if he could start repairs on the plumbing. She told him she can't hire him, as he doesn't have a work visa. He said he'd do it for free."

"Doesn't matter," I said. "That would still take the job away from a local."

"She told him that."

"Next time you come for a visit, maybe you should come alone."

"He did enjoy Thanksgiving at Marlene's cottage," Mom said. "They enjoyed having us. They got a new deck out of the visit."

I chuckled and stood up. It was too hot sitting in the sun in my dark uniform.

At that moment Dad came around the corner. I could tell by the look on his face that he hadn't found his friend.

"No luck?" Mom said.

"He hasn't been into the bar he likes for a

couple of days. I asked Darlene for his contact info back in Canada."

"Why would you do that?" Mom asked.

"I want to check with his family. He's a widower, but he has two kids. Maybe he told them where he's gone."

"I trust Darlene didn't give it to you," I said.

"No. She said it's private." He looked at me. "Could you—"

"No," I said. If I'd gone off for a couple of days with a new boyfriend, I sure wouldn't want some nosy neighbor calling my mother.

Dad dropped into a lounge chair. He looked like a total tourist. Bermuda shorts. Blue-and-orange shirt. White socks in sandals. Bright-pink nose.

"Come on, Dad," I said. "You're in one of the most beautiful places in the world, and you're making yourself sad. You said he's a widower. If Paul met a nice woman and went away for a few days, that's a good thing. Maybe he turned his phone off. Some people do that when they want to get away."

"Maybe," he said. "I know it's not really my business. It's just…it's because he's a recent widower that I'm worried, honey-bunch. His wife died a couple of months ago, and he says he's lost without her. He came here to get justice for her, he said. I don't know what that means. I'm afraid he's done something foolish. Or is going to. If I can't find him."

THREE

"HOW'S THE VISIT with the folks going?" Simon, the man who drives my ambulance, asked me on Friday.

I groaned.

"That bad, eh?" he said. "Wouldn't want my mama moving in with me, I can tell you that. 'Pick up your socks, Simon.' 'Where you goin', Simon?' All the day long."

We were in the ambulance, which we call The Beast, heading back to the station after dropping a patient at the hospital. A motor-cycle had come out the worse for wear after a collision with a van. Fortunately, the cyclist had been wearing his helmet, and all he had to show for it was a broken arm.

"It's not my mom," I said. "I get on great with my mom. She's really enjoying herself. Last night she made spaghetti the way I remember it from when I was a kid."

"Yeah," Simon said. "I can put up with a lot of naggin' once my mama starts cookin'."

"My dad's not having a good time. He likes to be kept busy, and there's not much for him to do here."

"Maybe he needs to meet some people," Simon said.

"But I don't know many people." I'd made a few friends here, but they were mostly women of my age. Not people my dad would have a lot in common with.

"I'm going out with my brothers tonight.

Why don't your dad come along?"

"With you?"

"Why not? See some real island nightlife."

"He might like that," I said. "If you promise not to go anywhere too shady or get him home too late."

"You the mama or the daughter, Ashley?"

I was saved from answering by the radio. Body on the beach. Police on their way. I told dispatch we'd get it, and Simon slapped on the lights and sirens. The dispatcher had said Code 5, meaning the person was obviously dead, but dispatch had been wrong before. Besides, Simon liked to pretend every call was an emergency. Maybe he hoped one of his girlfriends would see him speeding to the scene.

Our destination was Smugglers' Point, a small bay about ten kilometers from the main beaches. The ground was rocky, and cliffs on either side of the narrow bay made a dangerous ripcurrent. Too dangerous for swimming. The few people who came here would be hiking along the shore or looking for shells and sea creatures in the tidal pools. Two cars lined the dirt road, as well as police vehicles. Simon pulled in behind a marked SUV.

I jumped out of the ambulance and grabbed my equipment bag. A narrow path, sandy and covered with beach grasses, wound between the high stone bluffs. I recognized the young policewoman guarding the path, keeping the curious away. She nodded politely to me, blushed at the sight of Simon and let us through.

Sergeant Alan Westbrook crouched at the sea's edge. Water soaked his boots and the hems of his pants. The tide was coming in, and most of the narrow gap between the cliffs was underwater. A man and a woman dressed in bike shorts and hiking boots sat on a rocky ledge. Their arms were wrapped around each other. The woman looked at me, and I could see that her eyes were red and wet.

Alan pushed himself to his feet and turned to face us.

The body was half on land. The legs and feet moved with the incoming current. I took a deep breath and braced myself. Bodies that have been in the water for a while are not pleasant.

Alan stepped aside.

This one wasn't too bad. He hadn't been in the water long. He was a white man. His eyes were closed, and seaweed was tangled in his curly gray hair. His arms and bare legs were covered in scratches, but the ocean had washed the blood away. He wore khaki pants and a white T-shirt, gray socks and one running shoe. The clothes showed signs of being torn on the rocks.

I sucked in a breath. "I know him. His name's Paul Saunders, and he's staying at the Ocean Breeze Hotel."

FOUR

THE CORONER'S VAN arrived not long after
us. I'd quickly checked Paul's body, searching
for signs of life, but I'd known I was wasting
my time. At a guess, and it was just a guess,
he'd been dead for about a day.

Alan walked over to the young couple
who'd found the body. They talked in low
voices, but I got most of it. They were here
for a week's vacation. They'd been climbing
on the rocks and seen something in the water,

taking it for a shark at first. When they realized it was a person, they'd waded in and pulled him to shore. Then they'd called 9-1-1. They'd never seen the man before. Alan took down their contact information and told them they could go. Simon wandered back to the road, probably hoping to flirt with the pretty young policewoman.

The coroner's van arrived to take the body to the morgue. We stood in respectful silence as they loaded it onto their stretcher. Two seagulls settled on the top of the cliff to watch.

"I'm going to the Ocean Breeze, Ashley," Alan said once we were alone. "Darlene should have his contact information. I hate making this sort of call, but it has to be done. You said you knew him?"

"I only met him once for about a minute."

"Can you tell anything about cause of death? Other than drowning, I mean."

"No obvious signs of foul play, if that's what you mean. He hasn't been in the water long, but long enough for the fish and the rocks to start to do some damage."

"They'll do an autopsy to see if there's more to it," Alan said. "On first look I'd say it's an accident. He might have been alone on the rocks, tripped and fell in. Here or farther up the beach. It happens."

"I know it does." We'd had a drowning not far from here the previous month. The rocks are wet, slippery and dangerous. The water rushes between the cliffs, and the undertow is strong. People on vacation aren't always paying attention. "It might not have been an accident though."

"What do you mean?" Alan asked.

"My dad said Paul was a recent widower and was having a hard time dealing with his loss." I thought about how concerned Dad had been about his new friend.

"You think he might have killed himself?"

"I think it's a possibility."

"I'll have a talk with your dad. As you don't have to do the transport, want to come with me?"

"Sure."

I headed for the ambulance. Simon and I would follow Alan to the Ocean Breeze. As I reached the path to the road, I glanced back at the rocky beach. A huge cruise ship passed in the far distance. A small plane flew low overhead, and a sailboat skimmed over the waves. The sea rushed toward land, throwing up a white spray as it hit the rocks. Alan stood in the surf, gazing out to sea.

* * *

We found Darlene making a fresh pot of coffee. Alan told her what had happened but gave no details. She shook her head sadly and turned to her computer to look up Paul Saunders's contact information.

"Thanks," Alan said. "I'll call this number when I'm back at the office."

"I don't suppose you saw my parents today?" I asked her. "I called but got no answer."

"As it happens I did. They took the path to the beach about an hour ago."

"Thanks. I'll be back in a couple of minutes, Simon."

He shrugged and turned to Darlene. "So, Darlene," he said as Alan and I left the office. "How's your cousin Mira these days? Back from New York?"

"If she was, Simon, you'd be the last person I'd tell," Darlene said. Simon is in his late fifties, married with five grown children. He's never let that interfere with his pursuit of an attractive woman.

All the beaches on the island are public, but each hotel puts out its own umbrellas and chairs for its guests to use. It was January, the height of the tourist season. But the beaches here are miles and miles of pure white sand and shallow turquoise water, so no section is ever crowded. We found my parents relaxing on lounge chairs. Mom was sitting in the sun, a big hat on her head, sunglasses on her face, her nose in a book. Dad snoozed under an umbrella.

My mother looked up when I blocked the sun. "Good heavens, Ashley. What are you doing here in the middle of the day? And wearing your uniform. Aren't you hot? Alan? Is something the matter?"

My father grunted and started awake. He blinked at me. "What's happening?"

"I'm sorry, Dad," I said. "But we found your friend Paul."

"That's good, isn't it? Oh. No, it's not good."

"No," Alan said. "He drowned. I'm sorry."

"Drowned?" Dad looked out to sea. The ocean was calm and the surf gentle. Children splashed in the shallows. A young couple walked past, holding hands. "How is that possible?"

"Ashley tells me Paul was recently widowed," Alan said. "Would you say he was depressed?"

"Depressed? No. He talked about his wife. Told me how much he missed her." He glanced at my mother. The look he gave her was so tender, so loving, that I forgave him for all the times he annoyed me. She took his hand in hers.

"You were worried about him, Dad," I said.

"Yeah, I suppose I was," my father said. "But not that he'd kill himself. He wasn't like that. Yeah, I only met the man once. We had a couple of beers. Talked about the Blue Jays' prospects for this year. He was sad, but not like that."

"Hard to know what someone's thinking," I said. "He must have been very lonely, here by himself."

Dad shook his head. "He wasn't on the island for a vacation."

"Then why was he here?" Alan asked.

"He was looking for justice," Dad said. "That's what he told me."

"Do you know what he meant by that?" Alan asked.

"I asked him. 'Justice' is all he would say. He might have been about to tell me more, but one of the gardeners arrived to sweep the path. No, Paul didn't kill himself. I'm sure of it."

FIVE

I HAD SATURDAY off. I'd planned to take my parents to visit another island for the day. We'd catch a ferry, and I'd arranged a car rental for when we got there. Lesser Victoria is small and largely uninhabited. It is the Caribbean the way it might have been thirty years ago, before the big hotels and resorts arrived. It won't stay that way much longer. Small hotels are popping up. The big developments will soon follow.

We never made it to Lesser Victoria.

My dad had been sad the night before, after hearing the news about Paul. He hadn't slept well. My apartment has only one bedroom. I'd given it to my parents and taken the pull-out couch. I could hear Dad pacing in the hallway, trying not to wake me. He ran the tap to fill the kettle, bumped mugs together and dropped a spoon. I got out of bed.

"You okay, Dad?"

"Go back to sleep, honeybunch."

I yawned and hopped onto a stool at the breakfast bar. "You're thinking about Paul."

"He didn't kill himself."

"Maybe not. The ocean can be dangerous. People don't always realize that."

"He wasn't here on vacation. He wouldn't have been out exploring."

"Dad, you don't know—"

"Is Darlene working today?"

"She should be."

"What time does she get in?"

"Eight. Why do you want to know? I've arranged for a taxi at eight fifteen to take us to the ferry."

"Cancel it."

"I don't want to cancel it."

"Paul didn't have a car. We're miles from town. Wherever he went Wednesday, he went by cab. I intend to find out where that was."

"Please, Dad. Let it go."

"Can't, honeybunch. Paul wanted justice. He didn't get it. It might be up to me to get it for him."

"The police here are good. If there's something to find, they'll find it."

I might as well have saved my breath. I recognized that set of his shoulders and the tightness of his lips. My dad had made up his mind.

"How about a couple of rounds of gin rummy before your mother gets up?" he asked.

"Might as well," I said.

*　*　*

We were standing outside the hotel office at one minute to eight when Darlene's car pulled up. I was hoping she'd have nothing to tell Dad and we could catch the ferry.

"Good morning. Is something the matter?" She looked back and forth between the two of us. Her long earrings swung against her neck.

"Paul Saunders," Dad said, "didn't meet me for lunch on Wednesday as arranged. Did you see him that morning?"

"The police asked me this yesterday."

"I only want to know," Dad said. "I'm not interfering in the police investigation."

Darlene's eyes flicked toward me. I shrugged.

"He took a taxi," she said. "At ten o'clock. I know the time because I had just dialed in to a conference call with head office."

"You didn't see him return?" Dad asked.

"No. But that doesn't mean he didn't, Frank."

"Do you know which taxi service?"

She turned to me. "It was Henry."

"Isn't that the guy you always use, Ashley?" Dad said.

"Yes." And that reminded me that I hadn't called him to cancel our trip to the ferry.

"Great," Dad said. "He'll be here in a few minutes. We can ask him where he took Paul."

I caught Darlene's eye and gave her another shrug. Once my dad had an idea in his head, he had to see it to its end.

She went into her office, and Dad and I took seats on a low stone wall to wait for Henry. The rising sun shone hot in a blue sky. I watched a small lizard dash across the road and up a tree.

"Your mother will be disappointed at missing the outing you'd planned," Dad said. "But I'll make it up to her."

"How are you going to do that?"

"I'll think of something. Here he comes now. He's early. That's good." Dad leaped to his feet.

"Change of plans," he said when Henry had pulled the taxi to a stop. "You picked a man up here on Wednesday at ten o'clock. Do you remember where you took him? Did he say anything on the way?"

"What?" Henry asked. Islanders usually approach the point in a more indirect way.

"My dad's friend had an…accident," I said. "We're curious as to what happened. That's all."

"The guy who drowned off Smugglers' Point? Yeah, I already spoke to the police about him. I told them I dropped him in town and didn't see him again. He had my card but didn't call for a return trip. Was he a friend of yours? Sorry."

"Where did you go in town?" I asked.

"Stone Mills Center."

"What's that?" Dad asked.

"The tourist shopping district," I said. "We were there on Monday."

Dad opened the front passenger door and jumped into the taxi. "Take me there. Ashley, tell your mother we'll go out later."

"What about the ferry?" Henry asked.

"Not today. Let's go." Dad slammed the door shut.

Oh for heaven's sake! I wrenched open the back door and got in.

"You don't have to come," Dad said.

"Yes, I do. Someone has to keep you out of trouble. I'll call Mom on the way."

SIX

HENRY DROPPED US off outside Island Jewelers, the place he said he'd taken Paul to.

"Did you tell the police you let him off here?" I asked.

"Nope. I said Stone Mills. They didn't ask about a particular place."

Dad told him not to wait. He left me to pay.

It was eight thirty on a Saturday morning. No one was around. The shops were all closed.

The tourists were still in bed or enjoying a leisurely breakfast.

"Looks like we're too early," Dad said.

"I could have told you that, if you'd stopped to listen to me."

He read the small sign on the shop door. "They open at ten. We'll come back then."

I peered through the empty store windows. The goods sold here were valuable enough that they needed to be locked up overnight.

Two rows of shops lined the road. They were all painted a blinding white with navy-blue trim. The sidewalks were lined with palm trees, and each shop front had a giant urn overflowing with purple and white flowers. The shops were all upscale, catering to the tourist trade—art galleries, shops selling summer attire and beachwear, a real estate agent advertising vacation properties.

"Might as well have breakfast while we're waiting. That place on the corner looks open." Dad set off at a brisk trot.

"We already had breakfast," I said as I hurried to catch up.

"Another breakfast then." He pushed open the door.

The coffee shop was mostly empty. Dad ordered a bagel with egg and cheese. "Don't nag," he said, although I hadn't said a word. "I'm on vacation."

I asked for a latte, and we took a table at the bar counter along the window, facing outside. We watched as the street slowly came alive. More people came in searching for coffee. Shop employees headed for work.

"Ask your friend Alan how the police investigation is going," Dad said.

"He's not going to tell me!"

"Sure he is. He wants to impress you."

"He does not."

"Sure he does. I see the way he looks at you when you aren't looking."

My cheeks burned. "That's rubbish."

"No it's not. I used to look at your mother that way." He chuckled. "Come to think of it, I still do."

I scooped the last of the foam out of my mug with a finger and avoided my dad's eyes.

"Someone's in there," he said.

"In where?"

"The jewelry store. They're putting things in the window. Let's go."

"It's only quarter to ten. They're not open yet."

"They'll talk to me," he said.

I followed him out of the coffee shop. What else could I do?

I didn't believe for a minute that Paul had met with foul play. I doubted he was on any quest for justice. He'd said that to make himself sound important after enjoying a couple of beers with a man he'd just met. He was lonely after the death of his wife, on a vacation he wasn't enjoying.

I looked at my father, charging ahead. On a vacation he wasn't enjoying.

My dad was anything but lonely. He had a big family, a strong marriage, good friends, a loving wife. He was active in his children's and grandchildren's lives. Too active in my life.

But his job had been more to him than something to do. It had given him purpose. A sense that he was needed. I remembered how he'd rushed off to look at the plumbing in building two. He'd been proud to be asked. Wanting to be needed. Happy to help.

I caught up with him in front of the main window of the jewelry store. A woman was arranging the display—gold and diamonds on cushions of deep-blue velvet. She was in her early fifties, perfectly put together.

Carefully applied makeup, expensively cut and colored hair. She wore a peach suit, the skirt cut at knee level, the form-fitting jacket buttoned up. A gold brooch matched the gold buttons on the jacket.

She smiled at us. Dad waved. He went to the door and tried the handle. It was locked, so he knocked.

The woman tapped the face of her gold watch. Dad knocked again. I tried not to look *too* embarrassed.

Finally she unlocked the door and stepped back with a smile. "Thank you for waiting, sir."

"Not a problem," Dad said.

"Can I show you anything in particular?" Her accent was English and very snooty. I wondered if it was real or just the way she spoke to potential buyers.

"I'm looking for a gift for my wife," Dad said.

The woman glanced at me.

"Not me! He means my mom."

She turned back to Dad, dismissing me as not worth worrying about. I knew I didn't look like a woman who bought the sort of jewelry sold here. I was in a pair of beige capris, a cheap red T-shirt and well-worn sports sandals. All ready for a day exploring a remote island, not shopping for thousand-dollar earrings.

"I have something very particular in mind," Dad said. "I want a ring with six diamonds and four rubies. For our six granddaughters and four grandsons."

"I don't know that I have a piece exactly like that in stock at the moment, but I can show you—"

"My friend was in the other day. He saw one similar to that. He told me about it."

"Let me show you—"

"He was here on Wednesday. Canadian. Big guy. About my age. Curly gray hair."

"I don't recall—"

"Wednesday morning around ten. A taxi dropped him off outside."

The smile disappeared from the woman's face. Her eyes narrowed.

"Were you working then?" Dad asked.

"Yes, I was, but I can't possibly remember everyone who comes in here."

Dad looked around the shop. It was very small. "You can't get that many customers. It was only Wednesday. Three days ago."

"Oh yes, Wednesday. Now I remember. How could I forget?" Her light laugh was forced. "We had a plumbing emergency Wednesday morning. Water absolutely everywhere. It was a disaster. Total chaos. A few people came in around that time, but I was in such a panic I hardly saw them. I had to ask them to leave, as I had to close the shop.

"Now, about your gift. We own several shops, throughout the Caribbean, and I can call the others to see if they have exactly what you're looking for. If not, our in-house jeweler can—"

"Not right now. I'll try someplace else." Dad turned and walked away.

"Sorry about that," I said. "My dad's very particular."

I ran out of the store. My father was studying the window of the art gallery next door.

"Not very subtle, Dad."

"I don't have time to be subtle. If Henry told the cops he brought Paul here, they would have checked the shops to see if he'd come in. Funny she didn't mention that."

"Maybe she thought it was none of your business."

"I'm thinking this isn't such a bad place to live after all."

"What brought that up?"

"Lots of work for a good plumber.

Speaking of which..." He pointed to a white van parked at the end of the road. Big black letters printed on the side read *V&A Plumbing*.

The rear doors were open, and a man jumped out as we walked up. I got a glimpse of a jumble of pipes and hoses and toolboxes.

"Mornin'," he said with an island accent.

"Good morning." Dad thrust out his hand, and the man took it. "I'm Frank from Toronto. Been a plumber for forty years. No job like it. Just wanted to say hi."

The man gave us big grins. "It has its moments. Tony. Pleased to meet you, Frank."

"You being kept busy?" Dad asked.

"A madhouse around here lately. Everything seems to have decided to go bust at the same time. Hi, Ashley."

I'd never seen Tony before, but I'd learned not to be surprised when people knew who I was. Islanders seemed to know everyone and everything that was going on at any given time.

"Pays the bills," Dad said.

"That it does." Tony shifted his equipment belt. "Better get to it. Nice meeting you, Frank."

"A quick question, if you don't mind," Dad said. "That jewelry store over there. I heard they had an emergency on Wednesday."

"Yeah, they did. A pipe broke in the washroom. Flooded it and the shop next door. Catherine, the lady what works there sometimes, was havin' a purple fit. She can be a right drama queen, if you know what I mean."

Dad chuckled. "What time was this?"

"Ten thirty. I had to leave another job half-finished. You can be sure Island Jewelers will be paying through the nose for that."

"I'm looking for a friend of mine. He was in the store on Wednesday around the time they were having this emergency. She says she doesn't remember him because of all the chaos."

"What's your friend done?" Tony asked.

"Nothing, far as I know. I'm just wondering if you saw him. Big guy, my age."

Tony thought. "Yeah, I might know something about that. I didn't see him, but I might have heard him. Does your friend have a Canadian accent like yours?"

"Yes," Dad said.

"I was working in the bathroom. I finally got Catherine to get out of my hair and back out front. She opened the door, and this guy came in. He wanted to speak to the owner. Catherine said he wasn't there. He asked for the owner's home address. Catherine said she couldn't give it. He got mad. Started yelling at her. Insisting she tell him where he could find the owner. I started to get up, see if she needed help. She threatened to call the police. He left. Said he'd be back another time."

"That was it?"

"That was it. I finished the job and left her to clean up the mess. No idea if he came back or not."

"Thanks," Dad said.

"If you find your friend," Tony said, "tell him to go home. There's some people on this island you don't want to mess with."

"What's that mean?"

Tony adjusted his equipment belt and winked. "Hope you enjoy the rest of your stay, Frank."

SEVEN

"OKAY, DAD," I said. "I'll admit that you might be onto something."

"I won't say I told you so," he said.

We were back in the coffee shop. Dad had a slice of apple cake, and I had another latte.

"I'm not saying anyone killed Paul," I said, "but that incident does sound strange. I wonder if the police know about it."

"Why don't you ask them?"

"I will." I called Alan.

"Good morning, Ashley," he said. He sounded pleased to hear from me. I decided not to read too much into that.

"My dad and I are at Stone Mills. We've been...uh..."

"Trying to find out what Paul Saunders was up to the day he died?"

"Something like that."

"We know a taxi dropped him at Stone Mills Wednesday morning. We don't know where he went after that. Do you?"

"No, but we did learn something interesting about what he did when he was here."

"Okay," Alan said. "I'll bite. Not on the phone though. Are you still at Stone Mills?"

"Yes."

"Meet you at Corner Coffee in fifteen minutes?"

"As it happens, we're already there."

I put my phone away and looked up to see my dad grinning at me. "What?"

"Nice to have the cops on speed dial."

"We work together. This entire island has just one working ambulance, four medics and four drivers. Naturally, we meet the cops a lot."

"If you say so, honeybunch."

"I do," I said. "Let's find a bigger table."

The coffee shop was filling up with the pre-lunch crowd, but I managed to get us a table for four next to the back wall.

Alan soon came in. He was in uniform. It wasn't noon yet, but thick stubble covered his jaw and his eyes were red. He spotted us and came over. He gave me a smile and nodded to my dad. "Get you anything?"

"Coffee'd be nice," Dad said.

"Nothing more for me, thanks," I said.

"So," Alan said when he'd put the drinks down and pulled up a chair, "what's up?"

I told him what we'd learned from Tony the plumber.

His face didn't give away anything. He sipped his coffee.

"Is that news to you?" Dad asked.

"I knew Paul had been in the jewelry store, yes. I didn't know about any argument. The woman working in the shop said he'd come in and browsed for a couple of minutes. He didn't show any interest in anything and soon left. She thought he was killing time while his wife shopped."

"She lied," I said. "She didn't think you'd speak to the plumber."

"Don't make assumptions," Alan said. "This plumber might be making something out of nothing."

"Why would he do that?" Dad asked.

"He wouldn't be the first guy to try to make himself sound important to impress an attractive woman."

I was about to say, *What attractive woman?* when I realized Alan meant me. Flames crawled up my neck and face. He smiled at me.

My dad coughed. "I believed him."

"Look," Alan said. "I appreciate that you're trying to help. But there's no evidence your friend's death was anything other than an accident. If not an accident…" His voice trailed off.

"You think he killed himself," I said.

He nodded. "It's a possibility. I've spoken to his son. His son tells me Paul was depressed after the death of his wife."

"What did she die of?" Dad asked.

"Cancer."

"Tough."

Alan's radio spat out static. He held up a hand and leaned closer to listen. "On my way," he said. He turned to us. "Call from a hotel. Report of theft in one of the guest rooms." He got to his feet. "Sorry, but I have to take this. We've got two detectives off sick, and I'm all that's left."

"You'll think about what we told you?" Dad asked. "Paul was a nice guy. He wouldn't have gone into a jewelry store and had an argument with a sales clerk for no reason."

"Frank, you have to admit you didn't know Paul. You only met him once."

"I'm a good judge of character," Dad said.

"When I have a moment, I'll pop into the jewelry store and see what she has to say. That's all I can promise."

"Thanks," I said.

Alan gave me another smile and left.

"Let's go back to the hotel and meet Mom for lunch," I said.

"How do you find out who owns businesses around here?" Dad asked.

"The same way you find out anything," I said. "You ask an islander."

EIGHT

I HADN'T WANTED to get involved, but it was looking as though Dad might be right. I believed Tony the plumber. He hadn't been trying to impress anyone, least of all me, with his story.

Plus I hadn't liked Catherine, the jewelry-store clerk. She looked shifty to me. Not that I'm a good judge of character, as my recent failed engagement might indicate.

Neither is my dad. But he likes to think he is.

Alan and the Victoria and Albert police would do their best. I knew that. But I also knew they didn't have the resources to devote much more time to one tourist's apparent accident or suicide. Alan would be spending his time now clearing up the hotel robbery. The entire economy of this country is based on tourism. And tourism is based on the country's reputation as a low-crime, family-friendly destination.

The death of Paul Saunders would soon slip off Alan's plate.

I respected the fact that my dad wanted to get to the bottom of what had happened to his friend. But I didn't want him running off in all directions. Not in a country he didn't know. I'd handle this myself.

"I have to go to the restroom," he said. "Be right back."

I watched him cross the floor and disappear down the back corridor. Then I whipped out my phone and called Darlene. I kept one eye out for Dad's return.

In the three months I've been living on the island, Darlene and I have become friends. Not long after my arrival I helped her solve the murder of one of her cousins, a hotel chef. Darlene was born on Grand Victoria and has lived here all her life, except for some time away at university in Toronto. She is related to half the islanders. Her mother, or one of her many aunts, plays bridge or caters church suppers with the other half.

"Good morning," she said. "I hope your parents are having a good day."

"Sorry, but I've no got time to chat," I said. "Do you know anything about Island Jewelers? At Stone Mills Center. Do you happen to know who owns it?"

"Why do you want to know?" she asked, as I knew she would.

"No reason," I said.

"Of course you have a reason, Ashley. I'll guess it's to do with Paul Saunders. I liked him. He was quiet and polite."

"Did he say anything to you about what he was doing here?"

"No, and I didn't ask. I assumed he was here on vacation. He mentioned once that his late wife would have loved it here. The thought of her, I could tell, made him very sad." She sighed. "Island Jewelers is part of a big chain. They have stores all over the Caribbean. Both in towns and at cruise-ship ports. They're owned by a man named Claude Erasmus. Claude's grandfather opened one little jewelry store on Grand Victoria, catering to locals. When tourism began to grow everywhere in the Caribbean, Claude's father expanded throughout the islands. Claude now runs the company. My grandma used to work as a housekeeper in his parents' house."

"Claude Erasmus. I recognize the name."

"Everyone on the islands knows that name. And a lot of folks don't like it. Claude's into a lot more than the jewelry business these days."

"Like what?"

"Property development. Resort management. Some say his business practices are not always on the ethical side. Sometimes they skirt the law. He has a great many important political friends. Although *friends* might not be the right word. Step carefully, Ashley."

"I will," I said. "Thanks for this." I hung up and turned to see my dad approaching our table.

"What did you learn?" he asked.

"Darlene doesn't know who owns the store. But her aunt...uh...once owned an art gallery in Stone Mills, so she'll ask her." I jumped up. "Let's go. I'll call Mom and tell her we'll join her for lunch. She'll be wondering where we are."

My dad gave me *that* look. The one he used to give me when I was late getting home from "studying" at a friend's house. I gave him my sweetest smile in return. The one I'd used in high school to say, "I am *totally* innocent."

I did not want my father rushing off to confront Claude Erasmus. As Darlene had said, Mr. Erasmus was an important man around here. I'd been to his house once. The ambulance had been called. A dinner guest had suffered what he thought was a heart attack. The guest hadn't had a heart attack though. He'd simply over-indulged in too much rich food and expensive wine.

I remembered the house. It would be hard not to. All sparkling glass and weathered stone. A dinner party had been underway around the pool. A huge blue infinity pool set into the side of the cliff, with an incredible view out to sea. Tables on the patio, covered in crisp

white cloths, sparkling crystal, polished flat-
ware. Candles flickering in the dark. Golden
light spilling out from the house. In this job
I see a lot of different places, and I've been
to some nice houses. The Erasmus home had
really impressed me.

I didn't remember meeting Claude
Erasmus or his wife, if he had one, that
night. We weren't there long and didn't have
a chance to see much. Security guards had
escorted Simon and me to the location of the
party and our patient.

I convinced myself I was saving my father
from wasting his time. Claude Erasmus
wouldn't know anything about Paul Saunders.
Erasmus owned a chain of jewelry stores. It
was unlikely he would know what went on in
one of them with one customer. Still, I'd tell
Alan what I'd learned.

I'd forgotten how determined my dad
can be.

We grabbed a cab from outside the coffee shop and went back to the Ocean Breeze. We found Mom stretched out in a lounge chair, reading, on my small patio. She looked up at the sound of our footsteps and gave us a big smile. The vacation, I thought, was doing her good. Her skin had turned a light golden color, and a spark was in her blue eyes. My parents love each other very much, but trying to keep my dad out of trouble had to be mighty stressful.

As I was finding out.

"Any luck?" she asked.

"Luck?" I said.

"With your errand. About Paul."

"Oh, that. I have some feelers out to my island contacts. It might be a couple of days before I hear back. How about lunch out?" I said. "My treat as an apology for missing the trip to Lesser Victoria."

Mom put down her book. "I'll accept that. Frank?"

Dad grunted. "You two go. I've had enough running around. I'll make myself a sandwich and try to catch last night's game on TV."

Dad went inside, and Mom and I set out. We walked along the beach for about half an hour. We took off our shoes and strolled on the wet sand. The tide was coming in, and the warm ocean waves licked at our feet. Another perfect day in paradise.

We had a lovely lunch on a patio over-looking lush tropical gardens. Mom tried to find out more about Alan Westbrook, but I did my best to change the subject. I was paying the bill when my phone rang. Darlene.

"Ashley," she said. "I think I've made a mistake."

"What sort of mistake?"

"Did you ask your father to follow up with what you and I talked about earlier?"

"No. What happened?"

"He came into the office about half an hour ago. He told me you wanted him to check the spelling of the name of the guy who owns the jewelry store."

I groaned. "Don't tell me..."

"Sorry. I was on the phone with an unhappy guest and didn't pay much attention. I spelled it out. Claude Erasmus."

What's happening? my mother mouthed.

I rolled my eyes in explanation. "You didn't tell him where Erasmus lives, I hope."

"No, I didn't."

"Thank heavens for that."

"He called Henry."

"What?"

"On his way out of the office, he phoned Henry. They've already left. I should have called you sooner, but I've had a few things to deal with here. I'm sorry."

I threw money on the table and jumped to my feet. "Thanks for calling, Darlene.

When my father comes back, tie him up and throw him into a closet."

"What's happening?" Mom asked, aloud this time.

"Dad," I said. "Who else. Still determined to cause trouble. Can you walk back to my place by yourself, Mom? I'm going to run back."

Her face turned pale under the fresh tan. "Is he all right?"

"He's fine. He's gone off to question someone about Paul. He's interfering where he shouldn't. If he does learn something, I'm worried he's going to mess up the police investigation." I was worried about a lot more than that, but I didn't say that to my mother.

"Don't worry about me, dear," she said. "Off you go."

I set off at a good clip. It's not easy running on wet sand, and I've never been a runner. But I've taken up running since I arrived on

Grand Victoria Island. Mainly to give me something to do.

Believe it or not, a person can get mighty tired of the beach.

I was breathing heavily when I ran into Darlene's office. "Any sign of him?"

She shook her head. Her earrings tinkled. "No."

They'd been gone about forty-five minutes by this time. The Erasmus home was a five-minute drive from here. I called Henry, but it went to voice mail. I called my dad. Same thing. I left a message.

I took a seat on the couch in Darlene's office. Mom strolled up the walkway from the beach about twenty minutes later. She didn't see me and headed toward building one, where I live.

Another ten minutes passed. I jumped when my phone rang.

"Hey, Ashley," Henry said. "You might wanna get down here."

"What's happening? Where's my father?"

"He's okay. I'm watching him now. He's…
uh…questioning people."

"What does that mean?"

"I called my cousin Eddie. He's coming to
get you. Should be there in a couple minutes."

At that moment a battered old Toyota
Corolla pulled up in a cloud of exhaust.
The driver's side mirror was held on by duct
tape, as was much of the rear door. The back
bumper was twisted, and the right side had a
big dent. With no salt on the roads, cars here
don't get much rust. They just sort of fall apart
eventually.

"Does Eddie drive a once-red Corolla?"
I asked.

"That's him." Henry hung up.

I ran outside as Darlene called, "Good
luck!"

I wrenched open the front passenger door in
a screech of protesting metal. "Are you Eddie?"

"Yeah. You must be Ashley. Henry sent me. You can toss all that stuff."

I threw chip packets, soda cans, newspapers and several coffee cups into the back. I decided not to try to clean off the front seat. Obviously Eddie had a dog. A large, very hairy dog.

I pulled the door shut, and we took off. I would have clung to the door handle, but it looked as though it would come off at any minute.

"Do you know what's going on?" I asked.

"Nope. Henry said to hurry."

Eddie tore through the intersection. Approaching cars screeched to a halt. Horns blew. Pedestrians leaped out of the way.

I gripped the edges of my seat. Palm trees, white houses, tourists on bikes flew past. We hit the highway and traveled for about two minutes. Eddie made the turn on two wheels onto the road that winds up the side of the hill.

This is the most expensive area on the island. The properties are large, set far back from the road. The trees are tall, the gardens lush and the walls high. At Claude Erasmus's house, the tall iron gate was firmly closed. Henry's taxi was parked on the other side of the street.

Eddie pulled up next to it, and I jumped out. Henry gave me a wave. I leaned down and spoke into his window. "Where's my father?"

Henry pointed toward the Erasmus house. A window was set into the high wall surrounding it. A man watched us. He didn't look at all friendly. He had a shaved head and small eyes. He did not smile at me.

Henry then pointed down the street. A man and a woman were chatting on the sidewalk. The woman was large and round, wearing a cheap housedress. The man was my father.

"What's he doing?" I asked. "Who's that he's with?"

"I don't know," Henry said, "but I figured you'd want to know what's going on. Claude Erasmus isn't a man you want to annoy. If I'd known your father was going to cause trouble, I wouldn't have come here. Now that we're here, I don't like to leave him."

Eddie put the Corolla in gear and lurched off. He passed my father and disappeared around the next corner.

"What's Dad done?" I asked Henry.

"Frank said he had some business with Mr. Erasmus. I thought nothing of it. When Frank spoke to the guards, they wouldn't let him in. He insisted he wasn't leaving until he'd seen Mr. Erasmus."

"Maybe he's not home," I said.

"One of the guards called up to the house," Henry said. "He's home. But not interested in talking to your father. When they told him to go away, Frank started yelling, shouting for Erasmus to come out and talk to him. The guards said they'd call the police. Told me to get him out of here."

"Obviously that didn't work."

"I tried to talk him into leaving," Henry said. "To go back to the hotel. He said I could leave, but he wasn't going anywhere until he spoke to Erasmus."

"My dad can be mighty stubborn," I said.

"Claude Erasmus didn't come out," Henry said. "But his wife did."

"She spoke to Dad?"

"Yeah. I was here in my cab, you understand, so I didn't hear it all. But she was friendly. She laughed, smiled at your dad. Said her husband was off-island for a few days. Frank asked her about Paul. She said she knew nothing about him. If he'd come to the house, she hadn't been here, and the guards had said nothing about it."

"Do you think she was telling the truth?"

"I don't think that one knows what the truth is, Ashley."

"What does that mean?"

"The current Mrs. Erasmus is the fourth. She's…younger than her husband. Much, much younger. She hasn't settled well into the quiet island life."

I glanced at the house, at the watching guard. "What are you saying?"

"Emmeline Erasmus is an American. From New York, I've heard. She has quite the reputation on this island."

"Reputation for what?"

"She's a party girl. Loves parties. Loves giving them, loves going to them. Often without her husband. No one will say more, for fear of Claude, but there are plenty of nudges and winks when people talk about her."

"I can't see how that has anything to do with Paul Saunders. He's unlikely to have been her type."

"No," Henry said.

"I'll go and get Dad," I said.

Before I could move, my father trotted down the street toward us. He waved at me. I jumped into the cab next to Henry. "Let's go."

Henry pulled up beside Dad, and he got in. "What are you doing here, Ashley?"

"Trying to keep you out of trouble. It would appear I am not being successful."

"You told me Darlene didn't know who owned the jewelry store. You lied to me."

"So sue me." I twisted around to face him. "Dad, you can't go running all over the island interfering with people and accusing them of things. Claude Erasmus is very rich and very politically connected."

"I don't care if he's the prime minister's brother. Do they have a prime minister or a president here?"

"We have a governor," Henry said. "As we're still a British colony."

"Then I don't care if Erasmus is the Queen's brother. I want answers." Dad grinned at me. "And I'm getting them."

"What did you learn?" I asked.

"Don't tell now," Henry said. "The less I know, the better."

NINE

HENRY DROPPED US off at the Ocean Breeze, and Dad and I headed for my apartment. We found a note from Mom saying she'd gone back to the beach. Dad went straight to the fridge and got himself a beer.

"You can't go—" I began.

"But I can." He popped the cap. "And I did. Paul Saunders was at Erasmus's house on Wednesday afternoon around five. He asked to speak to Claude Erasmus, but the guards wouldn't let him in. They seem to have a habit of doing that. Not at all friendly."

"It's not their job to be friendly."

"Paul refused to leave."

I didn't mention that that sounded exactly like my father himself.

"He yelled and shouted and made all kinds of threats. The guards told him to go away or they'd call the police."

"How do you know this?"

"Neighboring maid told me. One thing rich people don't understand, Ashley, is that their staff often don't like them. They're happy to spread gossip when they can. If not about their own employers, then about their friends' employers. I spoke to a gardener from next door and a maid from farther down. The gardener was working on the flower beds next to the wall. He heard it all."

"*Heard*. It could have been someone else then."

"The maid saw Paul. She'd been at the store, getting ingredients for dinner. She walked by when Paul was kicking up a fuss. She made a positive ID." Dad beamed at me. "It was him, all right."

"And this maid just happened to be standing outside when you arrived today?"

"Of course not. I rang the bell and asked to speak to anyone who might have information. I didn't say I was with the police."

"But you implied it. You can't do that, Dad."

"The other houses on that street don't have the security Erasmus has. I wonder why he's hiding behind those walls and guards."

To get away from nosy Canadians, I thought but didn't say.

"Give your friend Alan a call. He'll want to know this."

I had to admit Dad was right. The police would want to know that Paul Saunders had paid a call on Claude Erasmus in the hours before he died.

"Did this maid see Paul leave?"

"No. She just walked by, her ears flapping, and went to work. Are you going to call Alan, or shall I?"

"I'll do it," I said. "But first, you can't be making a nuisance of yourself on the street, Dad. The guards at Erasmus's house would have been within their rights to call the police."

"I would have left by then."

"Henry said you met Mrs. Erasmus?"

Dad smiled. "Such a nice lady. Pretty too. She came out to tell me her husband wasn't at home. I asked her about Wednesday and she said she wasn't in when Paul called. She knew nothing about him or what business he might have with Claude."

"I'll call Alan now," I said. "Why don't you go and sit with Mom for a while? You're neglecting her on this vacation, you know."

"She doesn't mind," he said.

I didn't reply. I went outside to make my call.

"That is interesting, Ashley," Alan said. "I'll follow up with Erasmus. But it's unlikely to mean anything. If what your father's sources say is correct, Erasmus never met with Paul and Paul didn't go inside the house."

"Doesn't hurt to ask."

"No. But a word of warning. If I do find something we can take to court, the maid and gardener who spoke to your father won't testify. It's one thing to chat to a friendly stranger on the street. It's another to testify against a man like Erasmus or even one of his employees."

"Understood."

"Claude Erasmus has a younger brother, Pierre, who's been in trouble in the past. The sort of trouble a wealthy man can buy his way out of. I'll try to find out if Pierre's currently on the island."

"Thanks," I said.

"Don't thank me, Ashley. I'm not doing your dad any favors. But, once again, I have to ask you to stay out of this."

"I'm trying, Alan. Believe me, I'm trying."

* * *

Dad was even more restless than usual that evening. He wanted to be doing something, anything, about Paul's death. But he couldn't think of another thing to do.

That night I grilled steaks on the barbecue and then we watched TV. My parents were going home on Monday, the day after tomorrow. On the one hand I was sorry to see them leave. I'd rarely spent any time alone with my mother, and I'd enjoyed getting to know her better. On the other hand, my parents were living in my one-bedroom apartment. Not to mention the stress of trying to keep Dad entertained.

Alan called as the program came to an end. Mom was washing up the teacups and Dad was yawning mightily.

"Hi, Alan," I said.

Dad's ears pricked up. Mom turned around quickly.

I listened to what he had to say. "Okay. I understand. Right. I'll tell him."

"What'd he find out?" Dad asked.

"Are you seeing him tomorrow?" Mom asked.

"Alan went to the Erasmus house and spoke to Claude," I said.

"So he got in, eh?" Dad said. "That's good."

"Of course he got in. He's the police. He told Mr. Erasmus he was investigating the death of a man seen at his house the day he died."

"And?"

"And Mr. Erasmus was not home on Wednesday at the time Paul called. He was in a business meeting at the Blue Water Vista

Resort. A boardroom full of people can testify to that. Important, politically connected people. As well as hotel staff. He went from there to a private party."

"How does he know what time Paul called if he wasn't there?" Dad asked.

"Because Alan told him, Dad. And because his guards had written the incident down in their log book. Alan checked the log."

Dad grunted.

"The guards recorded your visit today. Mr. Erasmus told Alan that if you come there again, he'll have you charged with trespassing and creating a disturbance."

"Frank!" Mom said. "Don't you dare."

My father's eyes gleamed. "That means I'm onto something. He's running scared."

"He's scared of crazy old Canadian men bothering his household."

"I am not that old," Dad said, ignoring the crazy bit.

"And you have to stop bothering his employees. Erasmus told Alan you're banned from Island Jewelers and every other place he owns."

"I'm off to bed," Mom said. "If you get arrested, Frank, I am not spending the rest of my vacation money bailing you out."

"Might as well join you," Dad said. "There's nothing more we can do tonight."

"There's nothing more you can do period, Dad," I said.

My parents kissed me good night and disappeared into the bedroom. I unfolded the sofa to make up my bed. Before getting comfortable, I called Alan back. He'd mentioned that he had received the coroner's report on Paul. I hadn't wanted to ask about that while Dad was listening.

Alan answered with a smile in his voice. "What is it now, Ashley?"

"Just curious. What did the coroner have to say?"

"Paul Saunders died between eight and eleven p.m. Wednesday evening. Death by drowning in salt water. He'd suffered a blow to the back of his head."

"You think..."

"That might have happened after death, when the body struck the rocks. Impossible to tell. And before you ask, Claude Erasmus and his wife were at a party that night. They arrived at six and left around midnight. He wouldn't have given me that alibi if it wouldn't stand up. Your father's on the wrong track, Ashley. Paul fell into the sea. Maybe it was an accident. Maybe he jumped."

"Don't you want to know what he was doing at the jewelry store? Why he wanted to speak to Erasmus?"

"Sure, I want to know. But if Erasmus didn't kill him, it's none of my business. And it's definitely none of your father's business."

"Maybe one of Erasmus's employees did it on his order. While he was at this party."

"You and your father have given me something to consider, Ashley. Please leave it with me."

"Okay," I said.

Alan coughed lightly. "I've been pretty busy because of this illness that's swept through the station. But...uh...maybe we can have dinner one night soon."

"I'd like that," I said.

I hung up as a warm glow spread through my chest.

I read in bed for a while. I could hear the soft murmur of my parents chatting. They seemed to be arguing but keeping their voices down. I couldn't hear much. Dad was trying to talk Mom into something. She was resisting.

The only word I clearly understood was *jewelry*.

* * *

"Donna would like to do some shopping," Dad said over breakfast on Sunday morning.

My mother smiled at me. Her smile wasn't all that convincing.

"I thought you'd gotten all the gifts you wanted," I said.

"She wants something nice for herself," Dad said. "A souvenir of the island."

"Can't you speak this morning, Mom?"

"I want something nice for myself," she said. "A souvenir of the island."

I had a bad feeling about this. "What sort of souvenir?"

"A piece of jewelry," Dad said.

The stores on Grand Victoria open at twelve on Sundays. By the time noon came around, Mom was dressed in blue-and-white capris and a matching T-shirt under a blue linen jacket. She had on her best gold earrings and necklace and had put a big blue straw hat on her head. She'd taken off her wedding and engagement rings but wore her twenty-fifth-anniversary diamond ring. I, having argued until my face matched the color of her outfit, had finally given in. I couldn't let Mom go alone, so I also was nicely dressed.

We were, according to Dad, going to "poke around." To pretend to be interested in buying expensive jewelry. He couldn't go with Mom, having been banned from Erasmus's properties.

We took a taxi to Stone Mills and arrived at twelve thirty. As we got out of the cab, a change came over my mom. Her back straightened, her head lifted, she stared boldly ahead. She looked, I thought, rich. It was more than the clothes.

We marched into Island Jewelers. She marched. I scurried along behind.

The sales clerk pasted on a wide smile and hurried to greet us. It wasn't Catherine, who'd talked to Dad and me the day before. Her eyes flicked between us. Her eyes settled on Mom, and she gave her a beaming smile. "Good afternoon. I'm Barbara. How may I help you?"

"I'm looking for a new diamond ring," Mom said. "I want something suitable to celebrate my fortieth wedding anniversary."

"Your husband's letting you pick it out yourself," Barbara said. "Isn't that nice."

Mom laughed lightly. "Oh no, dear. I divorced him years ago. The ring is to remind me of my lucky escape. Although you can be sure he's going to be paying for it. Now, what have you got to show me?"

A spark danced in my mother's eyes. She'd had to be talked into doing this, but now she was enjoying herself.

Mom took a seat, and Barbara began showing her rings. Mom picked up a few, studied them, put them back. "I'm thinking," she said, "a sapphire in the center would be nice. Blue has always been my favorite color."

"It suits you so well," Barbara said. "Wait here, and I'll bring you a selection."

A few other customers entered the store. A young woman came out from the back to serve them. Barbara spent all her time with us. With Mom, I mean. Me, she ignored.

The range of rings was impressive, and the prices had me gaping, wide-eyed. But nothing appealed to Mom. At last she started to stand up. "I'm sorry, but I have a definite idea of what I want, and nothing you have is exactly right."

"We'd be delighted to work with you to design the perfect ring," Barbara said. Her smile had never slipped. "You can work closely with our jewelry artist. We can have it ready for you in a few days. When do you go home?"

Mom waved her hand in the air. The diamonds on her anniversary ring sparkled. She'd polished it before leaving my place. "I'm here for the season. I'm staying at the Club Louisa." One of the most expensive resorts on the island.

"Excellent." Barbara coughed lightly. "Of course, an individually designed and crafted item will cost a wee bit more."

"Whatever," Mom said.

"I'll call our designer now, shall I, and arrange an appointment?"

"I do want to get this sorted as soon as possible," Mom said. "I have a small… window…in which to send the bill to my ex-husband."

"Won't be a moment." Barbara picked up the phone and dialed. "Good afternoon, Emmeline," she said. My ears pricked up.

That was the name of Claude Erasmus's wife. "I have an extremely discerning lady here who wants the perfect ring custom-designed and made...Why don't I check? One moment, please." She smiled at Mom. "She happens to be free right now. Would that suit?"

"Perfectly," Mom said. "Once I've made up my mind to do something, I like to see it through immediately."

We were settled with cups of tea and magazines to wait for Emmeline. We hadn't even finished our tea before a little red BMW convertible pulled up outside and parked in the loading zone.

Emmeline Erasmus was a beautiful woman, tall and model-thin with smooth, dark skin, high cheekbones and huge black eyes. She was dressed all in white. Ankle-length slacks, white blouse, white jean jacket. Plenty of flashy gold jewelry and white sandals with four-inch heels. She crossed the floor in a few strides and held out her hand. Her nails were long and painted a deep red. Her smile was wide. "I hope you haven't been waiting long. I'm Emmeline Erasmus." She spoke with an American accent.

Mom made up a name. "Grace." She didn't give them a last name. "This is my daughter, Claire."

"Hi," I said. Claire is the name of my oldest sister.

"Now," Emmeline said, "what can we make for you, Grace? Just so you know, I studied art and small metal design in New York City. I have my own exclusive line of jewelry." I'd earlier noticed a display rack with a logo showing an intertwined EE. Nice pieces, but not quite in the price range Mom was—supposedly—looking for.

The next half hour passed in a blur of sketches and designs and chatter. Mom talked comfortably about gold and jewels, diamonds in particular. I had no idea she knew so much about rare gems.

Eventually they came up with a design Mom approved of. I thought it garish. I suppose that was the point. "A ring of this quality, with stones that excellent, will run in the fifty-thousand-dollar range," Emmeline said.

Barbara had been hovering the entire time. She jumped in now. "Why don't I take your deposit? Twenty-five percent now, the rest on delivery."

Mom stood up. I hurried to follow. "I'll have to think about it," she said. I'd barely said two words the entire time we'd been here.

"A small, fully refundable deposit will allow me to put a hold on the stones," Emmeline said. "Demand, as I'm sure you know, is always high."

"I'll think about it," Mom repeated.

Emmeline's lips tightened. "Give Barbara your details, and we can chat."

"I'm at the Club Louisa," Mom said. "I'll be in touch. If I decide to continue."

She walked out. I ran after her.

"That was awesome," I said when the door had shut behind us. "Where did you learn so much about jewels?"

"You remember when Claire was seeing that man from Oakville?"

"No."

"Your father and I never did like him. All flash but no substance, we thought. He gave Claire a ring, a very expensive ring. So he said. At your father's suggestion, I learned one or two things about jewelry. The ring was as fake as his smile. He and Claire broke up a short time later."

"Wow!" I said. "Fake jewelry. Do you think it's possible that's what they're selling here? Did Paul know something about that? Maybe he was involved?"

"No point in speculating, dear. Everything

she showed us looked perfectly fine to me. Not that I'm any expert. Call us a cab. It's time to go back to the hotel. I told your father this would be a waste of time. He was hoping they'd show me stolen jewelry, with a wink and a nod."

TEN

THAT DAY I was on afternoon shift, meaning three to eleven. Mom and Dad were due to go home Monday evening. Dad was disappointed that Mom hadn't learned anything at the jewelry store. Alan hadn't called with any updates. I left my parents debating where to go for their last dinner on the island.

Around seven Simon and I attended a call for a man who'd fallen down the stairs at his mid-range hotel. He'd had rather a lot to drink. After I did the hospital paperwork and Simon cleaned the ambulance, we headed back to the station.

"How's your new job going?" I asked. Simon had taken a part-time gig as a chauffeur. I didn't ask why. Simon always needed money. I figured it must cost a lot to maintain a wife and several girlfriends.

"It's goin' good. Easy work. Good money. Drive rich people to hotels and parties, hang around, talk to the guys, drive rich people home again."

Rich people. Parties.

"You ever drive Claude Erasmus?"

"Nah. He has his own driver. His wife uses our company sometimes. I've never driven her. Why you asking?"

"No reason."

"I've heard things about that Mrs. Erasmus. She's a wild one, they say."

"Do they?"

"Yup. Can't say for myself though." He chuckled. "Maybe someday."

"In your dreams," I said.

He chuckled again. "She's a looker, that one. Not too stuck up either, despite marrying into the richest family on the island. She was at the party I was at on Wednesday."

He made it sound as though he'd also been a guest. "You were at that party? Did you see Claude?"

"Yeah. They arrived right behind me. She was wearing this white dress. It must have—"

"What time was that?"

"Six. Dinner-and-dancing affair."

Claude had told Alan he'd gone directly to the party from his business meeting. He could have swung past his house to pick up his wife. But it was an inconsistency in his account of the day.

"I don't suppose you saw him leave," I said.

"No, but everyone left at the same time. Erasmus's car was called for same time as mine. Spot-on midnight."

"Oh," I said.

"Don't know what she got up to though."

I sat up a bit straighter. "What does that mean?"

"Oh yeah, you can be sure we had things to say about that. She left the party around nine. I figured they'd had a fight."

"Did she go with their driver?"

"Nope. One of the guys was in the house, using the washroom, like, and he saw her crossing the lawn. Heading for the street."

"Simon, did you tell the police this?"

He turned and looked at me. "Why would I do that?"

"The police are interested in their movements on Wednesday night."

"No police came to speak to me. Besides, lovely young lady wants to have some fun without her tired old husband around, I'm not going to tell on her." He winked.

I let out a long breath and leaned back in my seat. So Emmeline Erasmus was not at the party at the time Paul Saunders died.

Did that mean anything? I didn't know. But it was worth finding out.

When we got back to the ambulance station and I had some privacy, I called Alan. It went to voice mail. I left a message.

✳   ✳   ✳

Simon and I were busy for the rest of the night. Rachel and Liz arrived in time to take over from us at eleven. I called a cab and went home.

Mom and Dad had already gone to bed. Their flight was at seven the next evening. I made myself a cup of tea and debated what to do. I knew I should leave it up to the police.

"Good night, honeybunch?" Dad asked.

I turned and smiled at him. "Busy."

He pulled a stool up to the breakfast bar. "We're leaving tomorrow. I'm sorry I never was able to find out what happened to Paul. He was a decent guy. You say the cops here are good, but they're busy enough with obvious crimes. Like everyplace else. Some things fall through the cracks."

I'd decided earlier not to tell him what I'd learned. But before I could stop myself, I said, "Emmeline Erasmus left the party early."

He looked up. "What party?"

"Claude's alibi for the time of Paul's death is a party. The police checked, and he was there all night. But I found out that Emmeline left without him. Around nine."

"Do you know where she went?"

"No."

"You think..."

"I don't know what to think, Dad. She's involved in the jewelry store. Maybe more involved than her husband is. She designs custom jewelry for the store's customers. It's possible Paul was after her, not her husband."

"We'll have to ask her."

"We can't ask her if she killed a man."

"Sure we can. If we do it the right way." He glanced at the clock on the wall. "Nothing we can do about that now. Let's get some sleep. I have an idea."

ELEVEN

AT TEN O'CLOCK the next morning, my mother called Island Jewelers.

"Hello," she said. "It's…" She threw a panicked look at me. She'd forgotten the name she'd given them.

"Grace," I whispered.

"Yes, this is Grace. I thought over what we discussed yesterday, and I have a few questions for Emmeline. No, I'm afraid that won't work. I'll be at the spa most of the day.

We can discuss it on the phone. Her number is...?"

I heard Barbara say she couldn't give it out. She asked for Mom's number instead.

Mom huffed in disapproval. "Oh, very well. If I must." She rattled off her own cell number. It was her Toronto number. My dad would have a fit when they got the phone bill. "My first appointment at the spa is at ten thirty. I'll be turning my phone off for the rest of the day. There are other shops I can visit, you know." She hung up.

"You are so good at this," I said.

"I do believe I am," she said modestly.

My dad grinned.

The weather had turned overnight as a storm moved in. High winds whipped the fronds of the palm trees outside. Rain pounded steadily against the windows.

Mom's phone rang. *That was quick.* She picked it up. Dad and I leaned in closer.

"Thank you so much for returning my call," Mom said.

"I was pleased to hear from you," Emmeline said. "I'm so excited about doing business together."

"This isn't about the ring," Mom said. "I have other business to conduct."

"What sort of other business?"

"You mentioned fifty thousand dollars yesterday."

"That was an estimate only."

"Let's make it a firm price. My price."

"I don't understand."

"Fifty thousand dollars or I go to the police and tell them you killed Paul Saunders. At nine o'clock on Wednesday night you left your husband at a house party. You met Paul. You argued. You killed him."

There was a long silence.

"Now," Mom said. "I'm a busy woman. I can meet you this afternoon. You pay me and I'll hand over the proof."

"I don't have fifty thousand dollars in cash," Emmeline said. "Not that I would give it to you even if I did. I have no idea what you're talking about."

"You can get it," Mom said. "I'm leaving the island this evening. I'll be at Smugglers' Point at three o'clock. If you're not there, I'll mail the photographs to the police."

Dad pointed to the phone. Mom hung up. They high-fived each other.

"I'm the child of a couple of con artists," I said.

"Do you think she'll come, Frank?" Mom asked. "I certainly wouldn't know how to get that much cash in a few hours."

"You're not a criminal or a killer," Dad said. "She'll know. If she can't get it, she'll offer to give you what she has and pay the rest later."

"You're assuming she's guilty," I said. "She didn't confess."

"If she's not guilty," Dad said, "she won't show up. And we'll make our flight home. Ashley, your turn."

I called Alan. It went to voice mail again. I told him it was important that he call me back. "If I haven't heard from him by the time we leave," I said to my parents, "I'll call the general police number."

Next I called Darlene and asked if I could borrow her car for a short while. She said sure without asking why.

I put on a pair of loose sweat pants, heavy socks and hiking shoes, then tied my hair into a ponytail. I studied myself in the mirror, thinking I must be out of my mind.

Mom curled up with her book in a corner of the living room, and Dad and I played gin at the dining-room table. The kitchen clocked ticked on. Rain continued to fall. At two thirty Dad threw down his cards. "Time to go."

"We'll be early."

"So will she."

My phone rang, and with enormous relief I saw that it was Alan calling.

"We have a lead on the killing of Paul Saunders," I said. "We're following it up now."

"Who's 'we' and what do you mean by 'following it up'?"

"My dad made me do it," I said.

"Darn right," Dad yelled.

"We're pretty sure Claude Erasmus's wife, Emmeline, killed Paul."

"What on earth makes you think that?"

I explained quickly.

"Ashley, you've got nothing," Alan said. "So the woman left a party early. Maybe she was bored."

"Except we know Paul went to her house the day he died. That gives you reason to investigate her movements, right?"

"Yes, it gives me reason. It gives *you* nothing of the sort."

Dad crossed the living room. Mom looked up, her face full of worry. He bent down and kissed her on the top of her head. He said something and brushed his fingers across her cheek. Then he straightened up and quickly left the apartment. Mom watched him go. I blew her a kiss and followed my father.

"My dad's determined to do this, Alan," I said. "If Emmeline doesn't show up at the meeting place, we'll drop it. If she does show, you can sweep in and arrest her."

"Just like that?"

"Sorta like that. If she gives us money, she's confessing her guilt. Don't you agree?"

"She might just want to get rid of you."

"You don't believe that."

"I don't have to believe it. All she has to do is tell me that's what happened. Without evidence I can't arrest anyone."

"We're trying to get you the evidence."

"Ashley, I—"

Dad grabbed the phone out of my hand. "No time to waste. We're going to Smugglers' Point. Meet us there." He pushed the button to end the call.

TWELVE

"I'LL DRIVE," DAD said when I'd gotten the keys from Darlene. "You get in the back and lie down."

"Why would I do that?"

"I'll talk to her. I'll have my phone set to record, and I'll get it all. If she tries any funny business, you jump out."

"Dad, I really don't think this is a good idea."

"Sure it is," he said. "Besides, the police

are on their way."

We drove to Smugglers' Point. It was raining hard, and the windshield wipers kept a steady rhythm. I lay on the back seat, as instructed. "Fancy red sports car parked up ahead," Dad said.

"That's hers."

"Don't see her though. Wait, there she is."

The car jerked to a stop. Dad rolled down the window, and rain splashed against me. I heard the driver's door open and close. "Good afternoon," he called.

The wind roared through the trees. Waves pounded the rocks. Rain battered the ground. I couldn't hear Emmeline's reply.

I lifted my head and peeked out the back window. Emmeline Erasmus was standing on a rocky shelf. The sea was at her back, the tide coming in at her feet. She wore a brown trench coat over jeans and hiking shoes. The wind tugged at the scarf around her neck.

Even if she was foolish enough to confess to murdering Paul, Dad's phone would never pick up her words. Not with all the noise around him.

I glanced back up the road, the way we had come. No sign of Alan or the police.

Emmeline turned her head to look out to sea. Dad climbed the rocks, heading toward her.

That was a mistake.

The rocks were wet and slippery. Waves crashed over them.

I jumped out of the car. "Dad! Stop!"

He didn't hear me. Emmeline didn't turn.

As my dad passed a wall of rock, a large dark shape stepped out from the shadows. The man fell into step behind my father. Dad must have heard him. He spun around. Surprise crossed his face. He lifted his hands. He took a step backward. To the very edge of the rock shelf. If he fell, it wasn't far down, but the sea was rough, the rocks sharp. And my dad isn't a good swimmer.

Emmeline turned and started to walk away. To take a different path back to her car. She left my dad between the big man and the edge of the shelf.

I yelled and then ran. I pulled out my phone and started snapping pictures. The wind whipping Emmeline's scarf. Her startled face when she saw me. The big man looming over my father.

"Stop! Stop!" I waved my phone. "The police are coming. I've sent them these pictures."

It's unlikely the big man heard me, but he must have read my father's face. He glanced over his shoulder. He saw me. He looked at Emmeline.

She ran toward me, her pretty face contorted with rage. "You! You threatened me. You're blackmailing me." She fell on me.

Her long red nails flashed. I shoved her away. My phone fell to the ground, and when I turned to look for it, Emmeline grabbed my ponytail. She twisted. Rage made her strong.

I gripped her hands, trying to pull her off me. Her voice filled my head. Her eyes were wild. I managed to glance in the direction of my dad. The big man had left him and was running across the rocks, coming to help Emmeline. He leaped from one rock to the next. His foot slipped, and he fell hard. His mouth opened in a scream, but the wind whipped the sound away. Dad dodged past him. The man tried to grab him, but something seemed to be wrong with his leg. He dropped back with another cry.

Blue and red lights broke through the rain. Sirens screamed.

I wrenched myself out of Emmeline's grip. "Give it up," I said. "The police are here."

"You'll pay for this." Her eyes blazed with hatred. She spat.

"Not as much as you will," I said.

"What's going on here?" Alan Westbrook shouted.

"Arrest her!" Emmeline shouted. "That woman attacked me for no reason!"

Dad reached us, breathing heavily, soaking wet.

I pointed toward the rocks. "That man was going to push my father off the cliff."

"He's my bodyguard!" Emmeline shouted. "He was protecting me from these two lunatics."

"Constable Wright," Alan said, "go and help that man. It looks as though his foot's stuck between two rocks."

"I'm going home," Emmeline said. "My lawyers will talk to you."

"You killed Paul Saunders!" Dad yelled. "You attacked my daughter!"

"I have pictures." I glanced around and saw my phone. It was lying next to a rapidly growing puddle. Before I could reach it, Emmeline moved. She swung her foot, intending to kick the phone into the water. Alan grabbed her around the waist. "Not so fast. Let's all go down to the station and have a chat. But first I'll bag that phone."

THIRTEEN

EMMELINE REFUSED TO go to the police station. Alan told her she could come willingly or be arrested. She huffed and agreed to come. Her bodyguard was not arrested, but neither were Dad and I. Dripping wet, we all went to the police station and made our statements.

"The only intelligent thing you did was call me before going to meet her," Alan said to me when it was my turn to be questioned. "I can testify to that, if necessary."

"What do you mean, testify! We caught a killer. Why were you so late getting there anyway? We might have both been killed. Dad would have been, if he'd come alone."

"Accident on the highway," Alan said. "We had to take a long detour. Mrs. Erasmus's lawyer is saying your father was trying to extort money from her."

I harrumphed. "If that were true, she'd have had no reason to meet with us."

Alan stood up. He rubbed his hair. "Go home, Ashley, and take your father with you. He's not to leave the island without my say-so."

I didn't like the sound of that. "How long's that likely to be?"

"I can't say."

"What happens now? About Paul Saunders, I mean. You aren't just going to let her go."

Alan's face cracked into a smile. "She's not under arrest"—he held up one hand to stop my protest—"but now I have cause to investigate her and her business."

"Her husband will use his political influence to get her off," I said. "That's not the result we wanted."

"Maybe not. One of his lawyers came down as soon as she contacted him. He got a phone call a few minutes ago and left the station rapidly. He told Mrs. Erasmus to find someone else."

"What?"

"Claude's cutting her loose. He's in a mess of legal trouble himself. Something about offering bribes to government officials. I've been told charges are coming on that. Plus, his brother, Pierre, has come to the attention of the FBI in Miami. I've been working with them on that. Claude needs to distance himself from any activities his wife's been up to. I've seen the pictures on your phone. It's obvious her hired man is threatening your father. She appears to be about to attack you, not the reverse. We have forensic accounting people at Island Jewelers right now. If there's something going on there, we'll find it."

FOURTEEN

AND FIND IT they did.

Not only that, but the bodyguard turned on Emmeline. Alan suspected he was instructed to do so by Claude Erasmus. The island grapevine reported that Claude had been about to divorce Emmeline anyway. He could no longer ignore the gossip about her. Any criminal charges against her would only strengthen his hand in the divorce.

I was stuck with Mom and Dad for a

while longer. Mom was delighted to continue her vacation, but Dad soon returned to being bored and restless. He wanted to know what was happening with the case. Alan refused to tell him anything.

He wouldn't tell me anything either.

Darlene came up with some small odd jobs that needed doing around the hotel. That gave Dad something to keep him busy.

A week after the confrontation at Smugglers' Point, Alan called. "Things are happening, and I have some news. How about meeting for a drink later?"

"Are my parents invited?"

"Yes."

"When can they go home? Please say soon."

He laughed. "Soon. See you at The Reef at seven."

Dad insisted on arriving at the restaurant early. We found a table on the sand, looking out at the ocean and the setting sun.

"I'm going to miss this view," Mom said.

The waiter arrived, and we placed drink orders. Dad asked for a beer for Alan. "So we don't have to waste time when he gets here," he said.

"Here he comes now," Mom said.

Alan was in civilian clothes, and he'd recently shaved. He looked, I thought, less tired than he had before.

"I ordered for you," Dad said as Alan sat down.

"Cheers." He took a sip.

"What have you learned?" Dad asked.

"Pardon my husband," Mom said. "He likes to get straight to the point."

"Saves time that way," Dad said.

Alan grinned at Mom and me. "The guy who was with Emmeline at Smugglers' Point is named Oscar McGraw. He works for Claude. Under Claude's orders, McGraw's telling us everything. He says he had no intention of killing you, Frank. Emmeline asked him to scare you off. I doubt that's true, but I have other fish to fry here."

"Meaning Paul," I said.

"Yes. Emmeline phoned McGraw from the house party on Wednesday evening, needing a ride. He picked her up and took her home. About fifteen minutes later she drove away in her own car. He says that wasn't unusual. She often skipped out of events her husband took her to. McGraw followed her. Claude liked to keep tabs on what she was up to. Their marriage, according to him, was only for show."

"Thus Claude's happy enough to leave her to sort out her own problems," Mom said.

"Yup. McGraw says she went to a bar in town. He didn't follow her inside. But once we had the name of the bar she went to, we could ask questions. Paul Saunders was there that night, and he was seen talking to Emmeline. They were arguing."

"Why would she meet him in a public place?" I asked.

"It wasn't the sort of bar we'd normally go to looking for a missing tourist. She would have chosen it for that reason. But mainly, I think, Emmeline was overly confident of Claude's protection. She was sloppy."

"Can you prove she killed him?" Dad asked. "Their arguing that night doesn't mean enough, does it?"

"No. But in this business, one thing leads to another. We canvassed the neighborhood. We found a witness, a nurse coming home after her shift. She saw Paul getting into Emmeline's car. It's a very noticeable car. Step by step we can build our case."

"Why?" Mom said. "I don't understand why Paul was searching for her. Or why she killed him."

"I called Paul's children in Canada again. I asked if their father had been to the Caribbean before this trip. Paul and his wife took a cruise a few months before she died. He bought her an expensive brooch at one of the ports of call."

"Island Jewelers," I said.

Alan nodded. "The brooch was custom-made. They placed the order and paid the deposit. Paul collected the piece at the next port and paid the remainder."

"It was made with imitation jewels," I said. Island Jewelers hadn't been selling fake jewelry in the shop itself, but the pieces individually designed by Emmeline would not have been worth what she sold them for.

"Yes. Which is almost certainly what you would have ended up with, Donna, if the sale had gone through. Good workmanship though. Emmeline does know her craft. I got a warrant to search her studio. She had a nice trade going in fake jewelry."

"Did Claude know about this?"

"I don't think so. It was her side business. One thing leads to another, as I said. We're talking to the police in New York City, where Emmeline used to live. She must have realized her marriage to Claude wasn't stable. Maybe she wanted an income of her own on the side."

"She could have gotten a job waitressing in that case," Mom said.

Alan grinned at her. "After his wife died, Paul gave the brooch to one of his daughters. She, the daughter, had it appraised for her insurance company. It was worth a fraction of what Paul had paid. I spoke to the daughter, and she regrets telling her father that. He became obsessed with tracking down the people who'd cheated him. Not for the money, the daughter said, but because he thought they'd cheated his wife in the last months of her life."

"Justice," I said. "He was after justice. For her."

"He went to the store where he'd first ordered the brooch and found it closed. I suspect he's been tracking Emmeline Erasmus ever since."

My parents looked at each other. My father reached across the table and took my mother's hand.

"You can go home whenever you want," Alan said. "But you'll have to come back for the trial."

Mom shoved her half-empty glass of wine aside and stood up. "That's so very sad. Poor Paul. I'd like to go back to the hotel now, Frank."

Dad leaped to his feet and fumbled in his pocket for his wallet.

"I'll get it," Alan said. "Would you…uh… like to stay and have dinner, Ashley?"

I opened my mouth, but my mom beat me

to it. "Yes, she would. She's been working too hard lately. That and running after her father. Let's go, dear." She tugged at Dad's sleeve. "We can ask the hostess to call us a taxi."

I felt my cheeks flush as I watched them cross the sand to the restaurant, hand in hand. It was totally obvious, to me anyway, that Mom wanted me to have some alone time with Alan.

"Your parents have a great marriage," Alan said.

"That they do. I guess patience goes a long way."

My hand was resting on the table. Alan covered it with his. "Sounds like good advice."

I looked into his eyes. They were sparkling, and a smile turned up the edges of his mouth. I swallowed.

"One thing I'm learning that I need around you, Ashley Grant," he said, "is patience. Do you want to eat?"

"Not particularly."

"We have the world's best beach right here, and it's a beautiful night. Let's go for a walk."

He stood up. He walked around the table and held out his hand. I took it in mine. He stepped toward me and put his arms around me. Before settling into his embrace, I looked over his shoulder.

Just to be sure my mom wasn't watching.

Acknowledgments

Many thanks to Ruth Linka and the whole gang at Rapid Reads for their work on the important goal of improving adult literacy in Canada. Also to Barbara Fradkin for taking time out of her own writing schedule to read an early version of this book and provide invaluable comments and suggestions.

VICKI DELANY is one of Canada's most prolific and varied crime writers and a national bestseller in the United States. She has written more than twenty-five books, from clever cozies to Gothic thrillers, gritty police procedurals to historical fiction, and novellas for adult literacy. Under the name Eva Gates, she writes the Lighthouse Library Mystery series for Penguin Random House. Her latest novel is *Elementary, She Read*, the first in the Sherlock Holmes Bookshop Mystery series from Crooked Lane. Vicki is the past president of the Crime Writers of Canada. Her work has been nominated for the Derringer, the Bony Blithe, the Ontario Library Association Golden Oak and the Arthur Ellis Awards.